Jakki Wood studied graphic design at Wolverhampton Polytechnic and gained experience as a designer in a community printshop before setting off on an overland trip of Australia. She has illustrated many children's books for Frances Lincoln, including the Animal Friends series (with Donna Byrant); *Fiddle-I-Fee*, a noisy nursery rhyme; two exuberant animal books - *Animal Parade* and *Animal hullabaloo;* and one enormous traffic jam in *Bumper to Bumper*.

For Lauren

First published in Great Britain in 1994
by Frances Lincoln Limited, 4 Torriano Mews,
Torriano Avenue, London NW5 2RZ

First paperback edition 1995

British Library Cataloguing in Publication Data
available on request.

ISBN 0-7112-0863-8 hardback
ISBN 0-7112-0905-7 paperback

Printed in Hong Kong

9 8 7 6 5 4 3 2

NUMBER PARADE

A wildlife counting book

Jakki Wood

FRANCES LINCOLN

1 one slow tortoise **2** two hopping hares

3 three flying ducks **4** four frisky foxes

5 five rascally, rollicking racoons

6 six swinging, clinging, mischievous monkeys

7 seven squawking, talking toucans

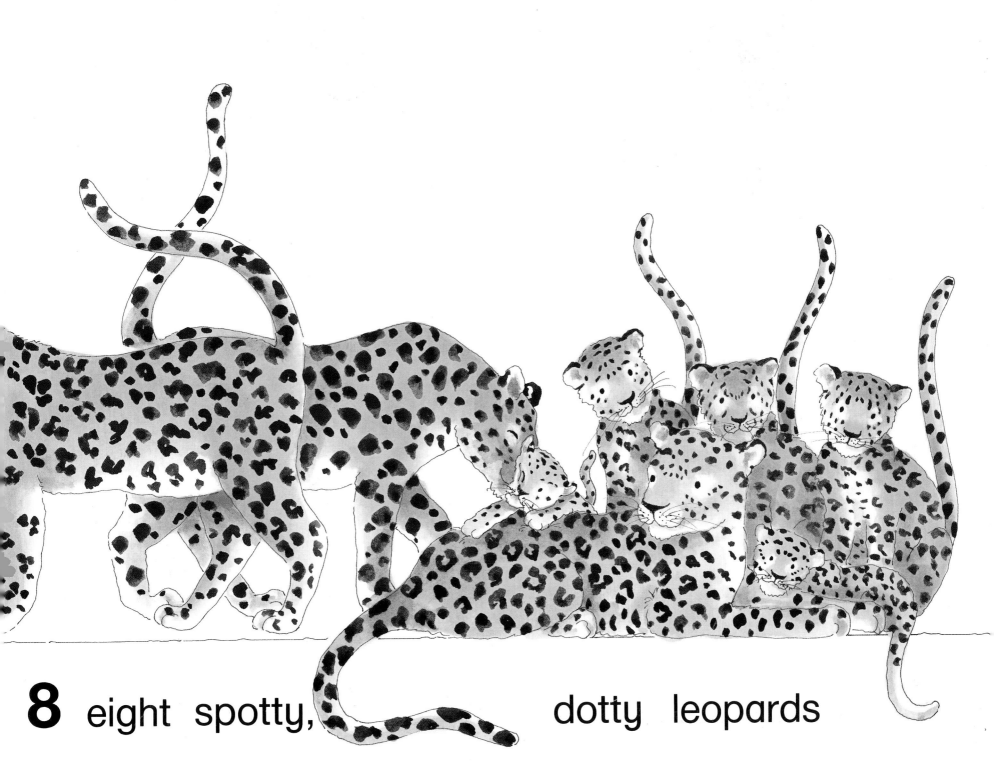

8 eight spotty, dotty leopards

9 nine   flip-flap,   slip-slappy   seals

10 ten bouncing, bopping wallabies

11 eleven   splish-splashing,

dip - diving dolphins

12 twelve   speedy,   gawky,

feathery, nosy ostriches

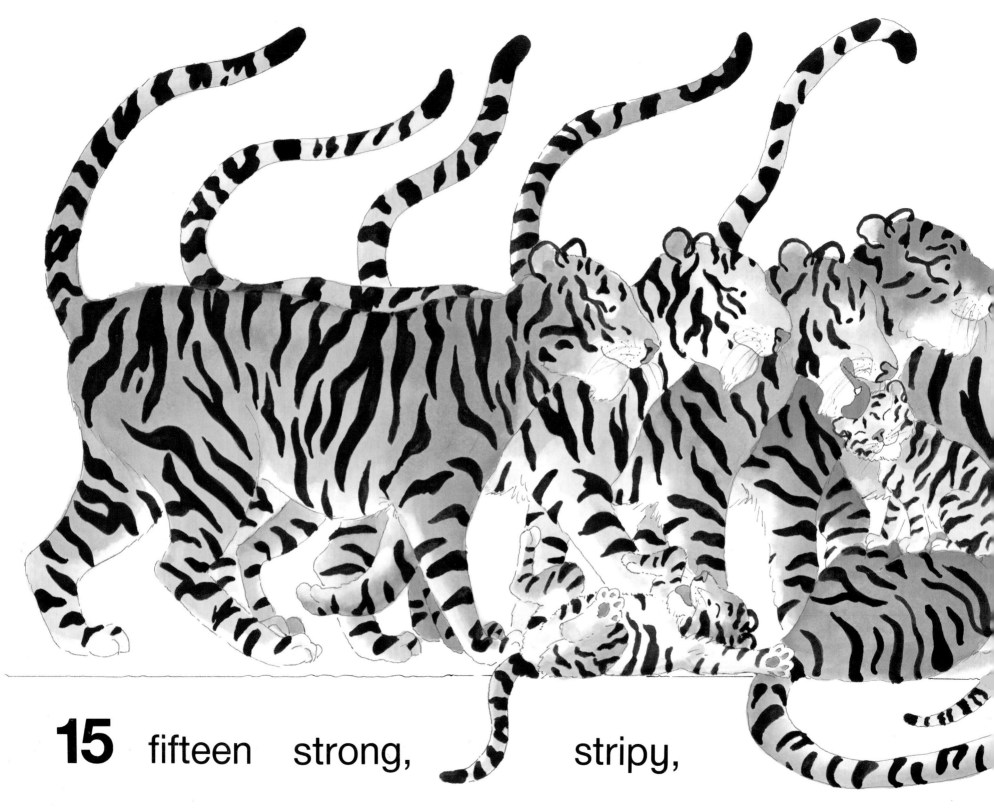

15 fifteen strong, stripy,

rough and tumbly tigers

20 twenty   hairy,   scary,   grizzly,

growly   bears

25 twenty-five humpy, bumpy,

lanky,   cranky   camels

50 fifty   lumpy,   lazy,   hefty,

hearty   hippopotamuses

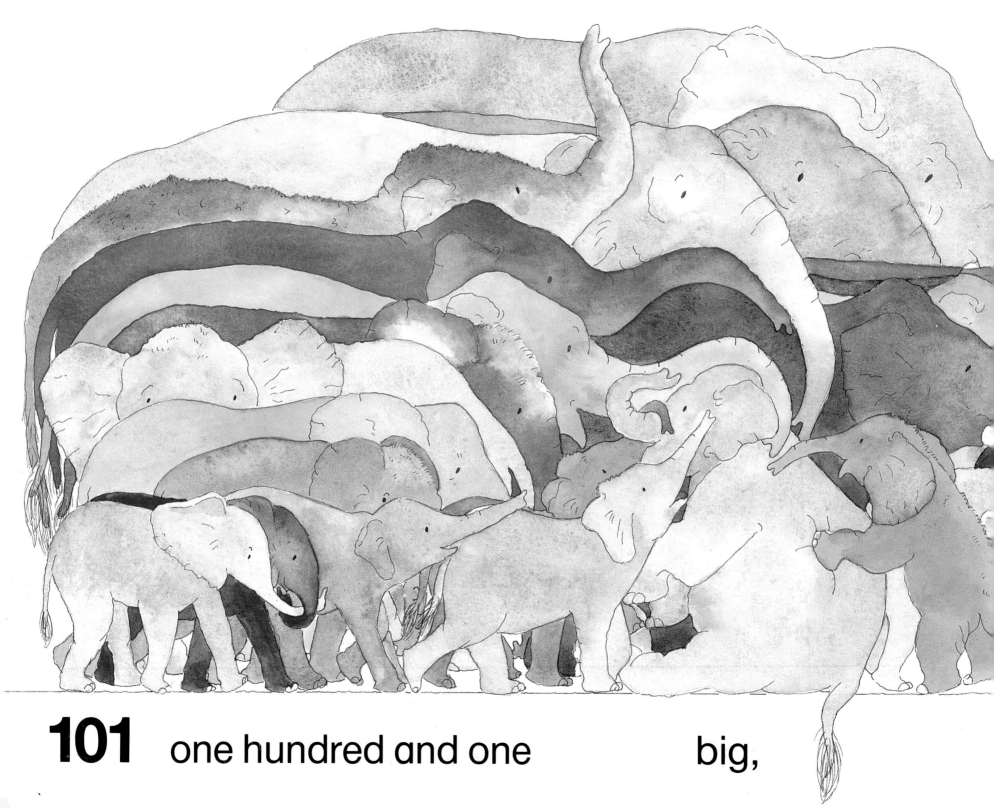

101 one hundred and one   big,

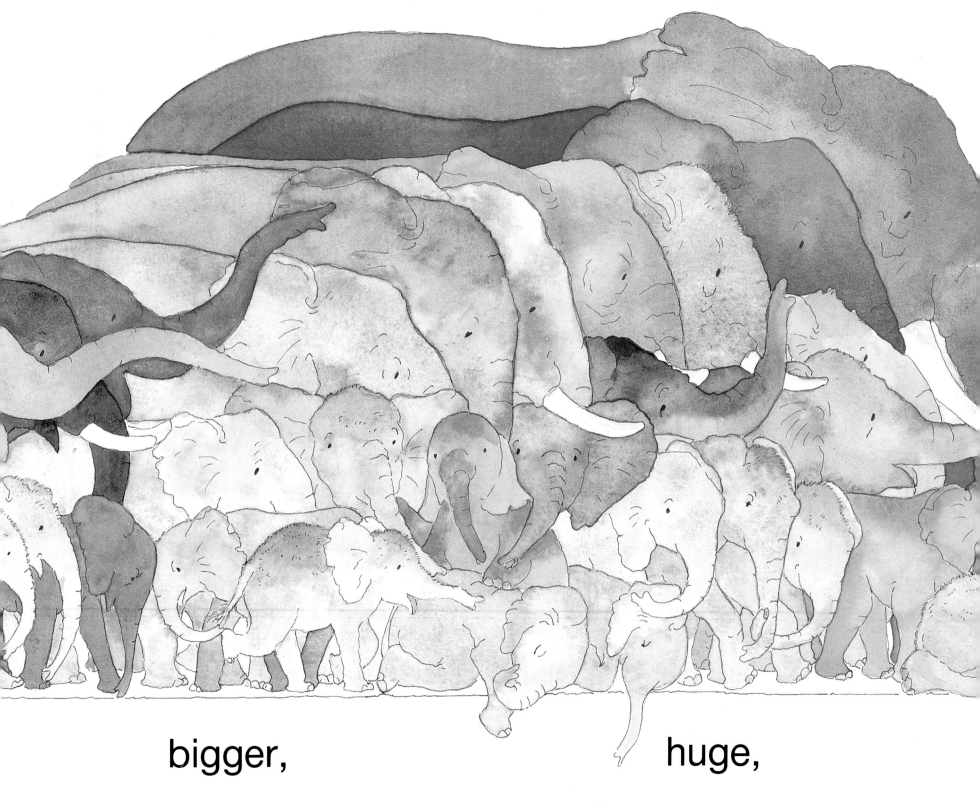

bigger,   huge,

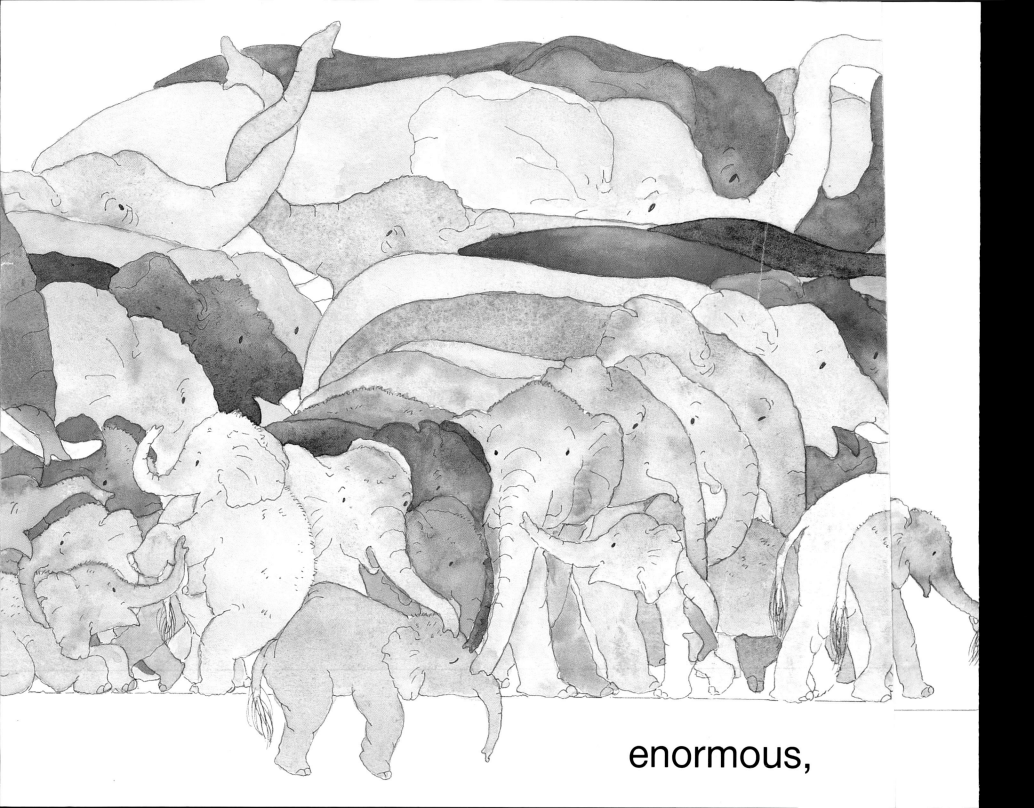

enormous,

elephants!

OTHER JAKKI WOOD PICTURE BOOKS
IN PAPERBACK FROM FRANCES LINCOLN

ANIMAL PARADE

Featuring a nose-to-tail march-past of 95 spectacular species, from Aardvark to Zebra.
Never has the ABC been such an adventure!

Suitable for National Curriculum English - Reading, Key Stage 1
Scottish Guidelines English Language - Reading, Level A

ISBN 0-7112-0777-1   £4.99

ANIMAL HULLABALOO

From dawn chorus to night-time call, more than 80 birds, beasts and reptiles raise their
voices in animated uproar, with a glorius hullabaloo of sounds children will love to imitate.

Suitable for National Curriculum English - Reading, Key Stage 1
Scottish Guidelines English Language - Reading, Level A

ISBN 0-7112-0946-4   £4.99

BUMBER TO BUMPER

In the busiest, liveliest, most enormous traffic jam you've ever seen, identify and learn
the names of more than 20 vehicles.

Suitable for National Curriculum - Nursery Level
Scottish Guidelines English Language - Nursery Level

ISBN 0-7112-1031-4   £4.99

Frances Lincoln titles are available from all good bookshops.
Prices are correct at time of publication, but may be subject to change.